KB020908

Arthur and the Scare-Your-Pants-off Club

For Tolon

Chapter

1

"I'm hungry," said D.W.

She was sitting in the kitchen, waiting for **breakfast**.

"Be **patient**, sweetie," said her mother. "Your father's almost ready."

D.W. **drum**med her fingers on the table. She didn't like to be patient. It took too long. And the only thing worse than being patient was being *told* to be patient.

"Just another moment," said Mr. Read. He was busy at the **stove**. "Lightly **brown**ed . . . a little **powder**ed sugar . . ."

"**Yum**mm," said D.W. She **lick**ed her lips.

"Yummm, yummm," said baby Kate in her **high chair**. She licked her lips, too.

"Don't take too long, dear," said Mrs. Read. "The kids are **rev**ving up."

Mr. Read picked up the **platter** and brought it toward the table. "Ta-dah!★" he **announce**d. "By special **request**, my World-Famous Whoopee Waffles. The favorite of **president**s, **professional athlete**s, and rock stars. There's whole-**grain goodness** in every **bite**."

"Whoopee!✳" said D.W.

"Now, if I could just have your plates, I'll be happy to **serve**—"

Arthur **rush**ed in.

"Morning, Mom, Dad . . . Gotta✳ run. Oops!✳"

★ **ta-dah** 나오신다, 기대하시라. 무엇인가를 처음 소개할 때 말하는 감탄사.

✳ **whoopee** 와, 야. 기쁨을 나타낼 때 쓰는 감탄사.

✳ **gotta** 'have to', 'must'의 구어체.

✳ **oops** 이런, 아이쿠. 실수를 하거나 놀랐을 때 쓰는 감탄사.

Arthur **unexpected**ly **collide**d with his father, **knock**ing the waffles high into the air.

D.W. **gasp**ed.

Arthur pointed.

But Mr. Read **sprang into action**. He caught the falling waffles on the platter, then **dish**ed them onto the table.

D.W. **clap**ped. "My hero!" she said.

Her father took a **bow**. "Lucky I **spent** that summer **wait**ing **on** tables in the Catskills."

"More," said baby Kate.

Mr. Read smiled. "I don't think so, honey. Let's not **push my luck**."

"Sorry," said Arthur. "I guess I wasn't looking where I was going."

"I guess not," his mother **agree**d. "But why are you in such a hurry?"

Arthur sat down to eat. "I have to get to the library." He **stuff**ed half of a waffle into his mouth.

"Slow down a little," said his mother. "Drink some juice. You don't want to **choke**. What's at the library that can't wait for waffles?"

"The new Scare-Your-Pants-Off★ Club book will be there today. I want to be first in line."

Mrs. Read was **impress**ed. "You're going to the library? On a Saturday? Of your own **free will**?"

"Wow!" said his father. "Hard to **argue** with that. But aren't you **exaggerating** a little? Are these books really flying off the **shelves**?"

"**Just about**," said Arthur. "They're really **popular**. I waited three weeks for the last one."

"Why do you think everyone likes them so much?" asked his mother.

★ **Scare-Your-Pants-Off** '너무 놀라 바지가 벗겨질 정도이다'는 표현으로, 본 책에서는 '혼비백산'으로 번역했다.

Arthur wasn't sure. "Maybe it's because they're **sort of scary** and fun at the same time."

"An **unusual combination**," said Mr. Read.

"Right," said Arthur. He **swallow**ed another bite and **dash**ed for the door.

Then he was gone.

"I don't see what the **big deal** is," said D.W. "But I think it's great that Arthur is going to the library."

"Why is that?" asked her mother.

D.W. **eye**d the platter. "Because," she said, "it leaves more waffles for me!"

Chapter 2

Arthur hurried down the street. He was thinking about the new book he would soon be reading. He **wonder**ed how he would get the pants scared off him this time. Last month's *Which **Witch** Is Which?* had started him **shiver**ing by the third page.

Arthur jumped high over a storm **grate**. He didn't want some **creature** from the Underworld rising through the holes to **grab** him. It was just that **sort of careless**ness that had **cost** Susie so **dearly** in *Night of the Cornstalker.*

Arthur turned the corner and saw the library ahead of him.

"Oh, no!"

Outside the building, a long line of kids had already **form**ed. It **snake**d down the stairs and along the **sidewalk**.

"Hi, Arthur!"

"Over here!"

At the end of the line, Francine, Buster, Sue Ellen, and the Brain were **waving** to him.

Arthur **trudge**d over to join them. The line was so long! It was **unbelievable**.

"Guess we should have met earlier," said Francine.

"Yeah," said the Brain. "Like just before **dawn**."

"Hey!" said Buster. "Let's not **jump to conclusions**. Who knows? Maybe they're just all here to study."

"On a Saturday?" said Francine.

Sue Ellen **yawn**ed. "Early on a Saturday?" she added.

Arthur **sigh**ed. "I don't think so, Buster. Besides, everyone I just passed is wearing a SYPOC★ shirt or hat."

"Even once we get in," said Francine, "there won't be any new books left."

"I guess we could **check out** some of the old ones to read again," said Arthur.

Buster **nod**ded. "Yeah. How about *Curse of the Mummy's Breath?* Talk about not **brush**ing your teeth . . ."

"Or *Skeletons in the Closet*," said the Brain. "I wore the same clothes for a week after I read that one."

The clouds **roll**ed overhead, and the sun disappeared.

"Don't forget the scariest one of all," said

★ **SYPOC** 'Scare-Your-Pants-Off'의 첫글자를 딴 약자.

Francine. *Zombie **Substitute** Teacher.*"

"Oooooh!" everyone said together.

They all **shudder**ed.

"I wonder why that TV truck is here," said Buster. He pointed across the street.

"Maybe the reporters are fans, too," said Sue Ellen.

"Or maybe," said the Brain, "it's news to see a line outside a library on a Saturday morning."

"**Never mind** that," said Francine. "Look! The doors are opening."

They all turned to watch. The library doors **creak**ed open slowly. A **sinister shadow** appeared within, slowly moving forward. The sun came back out as the shadow reached the steps.

"Good morning," said Ms. Turner, the **librarian**. "This is quite a **turnout**."

The kids **cheer**ed.

She held up a hand to quiet the **crowd**.

"It's a pleasure to see you all. However, I have some bad news. Anyone who has come to check out the new Scare-Your-Pants-Off Club book today will be unable to do so. In fact, all of the books in that series have been **removed** from our **shelves** until **further notice**."

The kids were **stun**ned. They **let out** a **shriek** of **disbelief**.

"I've been waiting for an hour!"

"No **fair!**"

"What happened?"

Ms. Turner held a finger to her lips. "That's all I can say at this time. **Naturally** you're all welcome to come in and pick out something else. But quietly. Remember, this is a library."

She went back inside.

The doors closed behind her—and nobody **rush**ed to open them again.

Chapter 3

"I don't **get it**," said Arthur as the kids walked away. "Who would want to **get rid of** our books?"

"Not all our books," Francine **remind**ed him. "Just the Scare-Your-Pants-Off Club books."

"Why **pick on** them?" asked Buster.

Nobody had a quick answer.

"Hey!" said Sue Ellen. "Look at that!"

She pointed to a TV store across the street. The SYPOC logo filled the screen.

Everyone **cross**ed the street to find out

what was going on.

*"In **suburban** Elwood City,"* said the news reporter, *"a parents group has **chase**d some children's books off the **shelves** of the public library."*

The picture showed the library and all the kids waiting in line.

"That's us," said the Brain.

"How did we get on TV so fast?" asked Buster.

"I imagine," said the Brain, "that they used a **satellite** downfeed★ to get these pictures back to the studio."

"Shhh!" said Francine. "I want to hear the rest."

*"The parents group, called PAWS—Parents Against **Weird** Stories—says the **scary** stories are bad for kids. We tried **unsuccessful**ly to*

★**satellite downfeed** 인공위성(satellite)을 이용해 텔레비전 방송 신호(feed)를 전송하는 기술.

SALSA
Eliza
5

*reach E. A. D'Poe, the **author** of the books, for **comment**. Hoping to build more **support**, PAWS is holding a **rally** for **concern**ed parents. They will meet on the library steps at one o'clock tomorrow afternoon."*

The news moved on to other stories.

"Red **alert**!" Buster **shout**ed. "If we ever want the pants scared off us again, we've got to do something—and fast."

"But what?" asked Francine.

The Brain **scratch**ed his head. "**Generally** speaking," he said, "**minor**s have **limit**ed **access** to **legal recourse** or **arbitration**."

"Which means," said Arthur, "that there isn't much we can do." He looked around at his friends. "But **I'm** not **willing to give up** yet. We've never given up before!"

"Sure we have," said Buster.

"Lots of times," said Francine.

"We're good at giving up," said Sue Ellen.

"Not when it's important," said Arthur. "Remember the time you helped clean out my **garage** so I could go with you to see *Galaxy Avengers?*"

Arthur remembered it well.

*Francine was carrying two heavy bags of **trash**. The Brain was **stack**ing paint cans, and Arthur was lining up two-by-fours* against the wall.*

*Buster was **sweep**ing the floor. When he finished, he started **balancing** the **broom** on his nose. Suddenly the broom fell off, **knock**ing over the two-by-fours. They fell onto the paint cans, which opened and **spill**ed paint everywhere.*

*Francine was so **startle**d that she **drop**ped the trash bags, and all the **garbage tumble**d out.*

"I remember that," said Francine. "Nice going, Buster!"

"It was an **accident**!" said Buster. "It could

★ **two-by-four** 2×4인치 크기의 목재.

have happened to anyone."

"The point is," said Arthur, "we **made it** to the movie."

"The *next* day," said the Brain. "After we cleaned up everything."

"Okay," said Arthur, "so we hit a few **bump**s along the way. What about the time Buster needed help with his **math**?"

*Buster was sitting on his **couch**, deep in **concentration**. His homework and math books were **spread** out around him. "Come on, Buster," said Arthur. "You can get this."*

*He and Francine were wearing the numbers 7 and 3 on their **chest**s. Pal was standing between them with an x, the **multiplication symbol**, **draped** over him. The Brain had an **equal** sign taped to his **forehead**.*

*"Think quickly," said the Brain. "My forehead is beginning to **itch**."*

"Twenty-one!" said Buster. "The answer

was twenty-one. I still remember it."

"See?" said Arthur.

"I'd forgotten about teaching Buster to multiply," said Francine. "If we can do that, maybe we can do this, too."

"I know," said Buster. "Let's go on **strike**! No more homework till we get our books back."

Arthur **sigh**ed

The Brain **fold**ed his arms.

Francine **roll**ed **her eyes**.

"All right, all right," said Buster. "It was **worth** a try. But who has a better idea?"

Nobody did—not yet, anyway.

Chapter 4

Just after lunch Arthur, Buster, Francine, the Brain, and Sue Ellen met at the Sugar Bowl.

"What we need to do," said the Brain, "is **quantitatively demonstrate** that we're not alone in our **opinion**."

"Huh?" said Buster.

"He means," said Francine, "we have to show PAWS that a lot of kids want their books back."

"I **wonder** where Muffy is," said Francine. "I called and left a message for her to join us."

"We can't wait for her," said Buster. "We

have to move, move, move! We have to **take action**!"

"I have one idea," said Francine. "We could get **signature**s on a **petition**. That's what my mom did to save the old City Hall building. If we can show the PAWS people how much **support** the books have, maybe we can change their minds."

"But it can't just be kids' support," said the Brain. "We'll need adults, too."

"Do we have enough time?" said Sue Ellen. "The PAWS **rally** is tomorrow."

"Well," said Arthur, "there's only one way to find out."

The kids **split** into several groups and **spread** out through town. Buster and Arthur **team**ed **up** on Arthur's front **lawn**.

"Gooooood morning, Elwood City!" Buster **shout**ed into a **megaphone**.

Two cars **whizz**ed by without stopping.

"**Step** right **up**!" Buster went on. "See the **Amazing** Arthur **perform feat**s of wonder! Then sign your name to save our books."

Arthur was wearing a **diving** mask and **bathing suit**. He was trying to **balance** on a rope above an **inflatable wading** pool.

"Buster, are you sure about this?" Arthur asked. He didn't feel very amazing. He didn't think he looked amazing, either.

"It's like a **commercial**," Buster **whisper**ed. "Before we can get them to sign, we have to get their **attention**. Now, **go ahead**!"

Arthur took a **breath** and started along the rope, balancing himself with a **broom**.

A few kids passing by stopped to watch.

"Easy, there!"

"Whoa! Back! Back!"

Arthur **lean**ed one way, then the other. As the broom **twirl**ed like a **propeller**, he fell into the water.

The kids laughed. "Again! Again!" they shouted.

"The Amazing Arthur will be happy to perform again," said Buster. "But first a word from our **sponsor**."

He pulled out the petition and explained what they were trying to do.

While Arthur dried off with a towel, the kids signed their names.

Meanwhile, Francine and Sue Ellen were jumping double Dutch★ in the park. A line of kids was waiting for a turn to jump.

Francine was **chant**ing,

"PAWS has taken our books away,
So I'm asking for your help today.
Line up now and sign your name.
That's the point of my rope game."

★ **double Dutch** 두 개의 줄을 번갈아가면서 돌리는 줄넘기 놀이.

As each kid finished, he or she signed the petition.

"Next!" said Francine.

Over at the bus stop, the Brain was trying to **educate** the waiting **passenger**s. He had covered a **blackboard** with **flow chart**s, **equation**s, and names of books.

"As you can see," he told the crowd, "we **predict** that the **impact** on school performance will be **geometric**. **Note** the **marked** rise in the learning **curve**."

He pointed with his pointer.

The bus passengers shook their heads. A few covered their ears.

"It is our **hypothesis**," the Brain went on, "that **recreation**al reading **yield**s many **educational benefit**s. Therefore, we **invite** you to sign our petition."

"We'll sign," said someone, "if you promise to stop explaining things to us."

"Yes, please!"

"**By all means.**"

"We **agree**."

They **crowd**ed around the Brain's **clipboard**.

He smiled. If everyone else was having the same success he was, they might have a chance **after all**.

Chapter 5

After Arthur and Buster had **collect**ed all the **signature**s they could in the **neighborhood**, they went to the park to **gather** more.

"Are you sure you don't want to be the **Amazing** Arthur here, too?" Buster asked.

Arthur was sure. He had been amazing enough for one day.

"Let's **split** up," he said. "That way we can cover more ground."

Buster headed for the seating area around the **pond** while Arthur **set out** across the fields.

At first Arthur had trouble **catch**ing **up with** people who were Rollerblading or biking or just playing games.

"Sorry, we're busy."

"Catch me later."

"Not now. We're at match point.★"

It was a little **discouraging**. He did **spot** an old woman **tend**ing some **plant**s near a **fountain**. Finally, someone who **wasn't on the move.**

He walked over to **introduce** himself.

"Excuse me, ma'am," he said. "Could I speak to you for a moment?"

"You already are," said the woman. Her glasses were **perch**ed low on her nose. "It's a little late to ask my **permission**."

Arthur **hesitate**d. "I guess that's true. It's for a good **cause**, though. At least we think it is."

★ **match point** 매치 포인트. 운동 경기에서 승패를 좌우하는 마지막 1점.

"And what is this good cause, may I ask?"

"A parents group has had our favorite books **removed** from the library," Arthur explained. "We're trying to get them back. But we want to show that a lot of people feel the same way we do. So we've started up this **petition**. Would you sign it for us?"

The woman **paused**. "I see I'm not the only one doing **volunteer** work today." She gave Arthur a long look. "It all **depends** on the books. I wouldn't want to **go against** your parents' wishes."

"Oh, you wouldn't be. My parents like me to read different things. My father says it's like the food groups.★ It's **healthy** to have a little **bit** of everything."

"Good **advice**," said the woman.

"Besides," said Arthur, "these books are our

★ **food group** 식품군. 영양 성분이 유사한 식품들을 몇 가지로 나누어 분류한 것.

favorites: the Scare-Your-Pants-Off Club books."

The old woman sat back on her **heel**s and pushed her glasses back up on her nose.

"Really? The Scare-Your-Pants-Off Club books? Do you read them . . . um . . . ?"

"Arthur." He shook her hand. "Do I read them? Of course! I haven't **miss**ed a **single** one."

The woman **frown**ed. "Then the situation is **serious**. Maybe I should speak to this parents group myself!"

She stood up and gathered her **garden**ing **tool**s.

"Don't **give up**, Arthur. You and your friends are doing a good thing."

Arthur looked **puzzle**d. "Sure. Thanks—I think . . ."

He watched her leave. Then he looked down at his **clipboard**. "Hey! Wait! You forgot to sign."

But the woman was gone.

Later that afternoon, Arthur, Francine, Sue Ellen, and Buster walked out of the Sugar Bowl, eating ice cream cones.

"**Collect**ing **signature**s is hard work," said Buster.

"Do you think we have enough names?" asked Francine.

Arthur **lick**ed the **drip**s around his cone. "I think so. There are pages and pages. I just hope PAWS will listen to us."

Francine looked at her watch. "I **wonder** where the Brain is. He **was supposed to** meet us at five."

"Look!" said Buster. "Here comes Muffy."

"Where has she been, anyway?" said Francine. "We could have used her help today."

Muffy was wearing a big smile. "Great news, everyone!" she **announced**. "My parents are having a big party tomorrow at WonderWorld." She **paused**. "And I can **invite** anyone I want."

"Wow!" said Arthur. WonderWorld was the best **carnival** and **theme** park around. Going there for free would be a real **treat**.

"That's **terrific**," said Sue Ellen.

"**Count** me in!" said Francine.

Francine **noticed** Muffy **eye**ing her cone.

"Want a lick?" she asked. She **held out** the cone.

Muffy backed away. "Um, no thanks. My mom won't let me—too much **fat** and sugar."

She shut her eyes. "Take it away. Please!"

At that moment the Brain came around the corner. He was **clutch**ing a newspaper in one hand.

"Sorry I'm late, everyone. Wait till you hear what I just—" He stopped suddenly. "Oh . . . hello, Muffy."

Muffy looked at the **sidewalk**.

"What did you find out?" Francine asked.

The Brain **glance**d in Muffy's **direction**. "Listen to this," he said. "There's a whole **article** in today's paper about the book **ban** and an **interview** with the people behind it. I'll **skip** to the important part."

He started reading from the newspaper.

"'*Kids don't know the **harm** these books do,' said Millicent Crosswire. 'My poor daughter, Muffy, read just one, and it gave her **awful** nightmares.'*"

Everyone looked at Muffy. She continued

THE SUGA
GIANT SALE
FAKES
OPEN 9AM-9PM

to study the **crack**s in the sidewalk.

The Brain read some more. *"'We started PAWS to save other kids,' added Millicent's husband, Ed. 'We're having a big **rally** for **concern**ed parents at the library tomorrow. **Afterward**, all our **support**ers—young and old— can join us for a **celebration** at WonderWorld.'"*

Buster was **shock**ed. "Muffy, your mom and dad started PAWS?"

Muffy looked up. "Yes," she said.

"But why?" asked Francine.

Muffy **bit** her lip.

"Let me see that," Arthur said to the Brain.

The Brain gave him the newspaper.

Arthur read through the interview. "This isn't just **any old** WonderWorld party," he said. "Is it, Muffy? It's only for people who support PAWS."

Muffy **shrug**ged. "Well, if you want to get **technical** . . ."

"Oh, no!" said Buster.

"We have to get our books back, Muffy," said Arthur. "Don't you understand?"

Muffy **hesitate**d. Then she took a deep **breath** and **fold**ed her arms.

"You just have to decide which means more to you," she said. "WonderWorld—or a **bunch** of **silly** books. The **choice** is yours."

"I don't know what's so **complicated**," said D.W. She put out her hands as though she were **balancing** things in a **scale**. "Some **creepy** books here. Free WonderWorld here." She **lower**ed her WonderWorld hand to her **knee**s, as though it was holding something heavy. The other hand **shot** up. "No **contest**."

She and Arthur were sitting in the living room. Arthur had told her about the problem with Muffy and her parents.

"It's not that simple," said Arthur.

D.W. laughed. "It is to me. You know

how great WonderWorld is. They have the best roller coaster. People **throw up and everything**. What do you think, Kate?"

Their baby sister was watching from her **playpen**. Her hands were going up and down.

"See, Arthur?" said D.W. "Even Kate knows the right thing to do. And she's just a baby."

"The right thing to do about what?" asked Mrs. Read, taking a **break** from her work.

"Arthur gets to go to WonderWorld for free," said D.W.

"Really?" said Mrs. Read. "How did that **come about**?"

Arthur told her.

"I see," said his mother. "Well, Arthur, for someone going to WonderWorld, you don't look very happy."

Arthur **sigh**ed. "As I was trying to tell D.W., it's not that simple. I don't want to **miss**

Muffy's party. But I don't want to lose my favorite books, either. And it's not really right to go if I don't **support** PAWS."

Mrs. Read **nod**ded. "It's a difficult situation, Arthur. It's like a balance **sheet**. There are pluses and minuses. When you add everything up, you have to do what you think is right—even if it means making a **sacrifice**."

Arthur **wander**ed outside to think some more. Why did **stick**ing **up for** what you believe in have to be so difficult?

"I wish I knew what everyone else was thinking," Arthur **mutter**ed.

"I'll tell you what I'm thinking," said his father from the **garage**. "My life's an open book.* A cookbook, that is." Mr. Read was busy with a huge **catering** job. But right now, he was looking through boxes.

★**open book** '펼쳐진 책'이라는 표현은 어떤 사람의 행동이나 태도, 생각 등이 다 알려져 있어 알기 쉽다는 의미이다.

"I wish there was a book where I could look up the answers to hard questions," Arthur said.

He explained the situation to his father.

"That would be a good book to have," his father **agree**d. "Probably a bestseller." He opened a box. "Ah, here's what I was looking for."

He pulled out a **clown costume**. "Just what I need for this afternoon's children's hospital **benefit**."

He began putting the costume on.

"What if I'm the only one who decides to **protest** PAWS?" said Arthur. "What if all my friends decide to go to WonderWorld instead?"

Mr. Read **adjust**ed his **bald wig**. "Can't be **afraid** to look **foolish** for something you believe in. Give me that **rubber** nose, please."

Arthur handed it to him. Then he sat

down to think.

Bllaaattttt!

Arthur jumped up.

"Oh, thanks," said his father. "I **wonder**ed where that whoopee cushion* was." Mr. Read put it in his pocket.

He looked at his watch.

"I've got to be going. Remember one thing, Arthur. I know you want to do what your friends are doing. But look at me."

Arthur **stare**d at his father in his clown **suit**.

"Sometimes clowns work as a team." His father shook hands with a **bunch** of **imaginary** clowns around him. "And sometimes they stand under the **spotlight all by themselves**." He made a little **bow**.

Arthur sighed. And sometimes clowns looked sad, the way he felt right now.

★ **whoopee cushion** 깔고 앉으면 방귀 소리가 나는 쿠션.

At the library the next morning, the Crosswires stood at the top of the steps. Muffy kept **duck**ing behind her parents, but they kept pulling her out in front of them.

A **crowd** of kids and parents was **gather**ed around them.

Mr. Crosswire spoke into a **portable microphone**. "Thank you all for coming. I'm Ed Crosswire of Crosswire Motors, corner of Park and Lakewood, open most nights till ten. But I'm not doing this for me. I'm doing it to save our kids!"

His words were met by **cheers** and **polite applause**.

Off to the side, Arthur stood with his mother. He was holding up a sign that said, KEEP YOUR **PAW**S OFF OUR BOOKS!

Nobody seemed to be paying **attention**.

"I don't see anyone," said Arthur. "I guess WonderWorld wins."

"Don't be too sure," said Mrs. Read. "There's still time."

"This is our little girl," Ed Crosswire continued. He held up Muffy's hand. "We started PAWS because of her, but we care about all of you as well."

At that moment Buster, Francine, the Brain, and Sue Ellen came around the corner. They were holding signs over their heads.

OBEY THE **LAWS**—NOT PAWS!

CLOSE THE BOOK ON PAWS!

"You're here!" said Arthur. "I was beginning

to **wonder**."

"Sorry we're late," said the Brain. "We stopped for more **signature**s."

He **held out** the **petition sheet**s. There were now **dozen**s and dozens of names.

"So who's going to give these to Mr. Crosswire?" Buster asked.

"You do it," said the Brain.

"Not me," said Buster. "You do it."

"Who?" said Sue Ellen.

"Not you," said Francine. "How about Arthur?"

"Yeah!"

"Good idea."

"Well, Arthur . . . ," said the Brain.

Arthur took a deep **breath**. "All right," he said. "I'll do it!"

Holding the petitions under one arm, he worked his way through the crowd.

No Ferris wheel.* No sno-cones.* No roller

coaster.

"Excuse me. Excuse me. Coming through."

No cotton candy.* No bumper cars. No **haunt**ed house.*

At the top of the steps, Arthur stopped in front of Mr. Crosswire. He would be sorry to **miss** all those great things at WonderWorld. But this was more important.

"If we don't **take a stand** now, we will have **fail**ed in our trust. We must—"

"Excuse me, please, Mr. Crosswire," said Arthur. "We need to talk."

"Not now, Arthur. I'm **on a roll**."

"**That's just it**, Mr. Crosswire. You're **rol**ling right over our **right**s. It's not **fair**. Speaking for the kids, we really want our books back.

★ **Ferris wheel** 유원지에 있는 관람차.
✴ **sno-cones** 원추형의 종이컵에 깎은 얼음 조각을 넣고 시럽을 뿌린 빙수.
✳ **cotton candy** 솜사탕.
✴ **haunted house** 귀신의 집.

SCARE YOUR PAWS OFF

We've got these signatures of **support**—"

"That's nice, Arthur. I **admire** your **spirit**. But believe me, this is for your own **good**! These books are trouble with a **capital** *T*.★"

"Have you read them?" asked a voice from the crowd.

Arthur turned around. That voice was **familiar**.

Surprisingly, it was familiar to Ed Crosswire, too. He looked out over the crowd. He seemed a little **confused**.

Arthur wondered what would happen next.

★ **with a capital A, B, . . .** 그야말로, 정말로, 진짜로. 특정한 단어의 의미를 강조할 때, 그 단어의 첫 글자를 대문자로 써서 나타내는 표현법이다. 여러 상황에서 다양하게 확장하여 사용할 수 있다. He was romantic with a capital R. 그는 그야말로 낭만적이었다. You are wrong with a capital W. 너는 완전히 틀렸다.

Chapter 9

"Who is that?" asked Ed Crosswire.

The rest of the **crowd** was silent.

"Answer the question," said the voice. "Have you read the books you're **condemn**ing?"

The crowd **pull**ed **back** to **reveal** the speaker. Arthur **recognize**d her. She was the woman he had spoken with in the park.

Mr. Crosswire cleared his **throat**. "I am proud to say that I wouldn't read these books if you paid me!"

The woman **sigh**ed. "I'm not **surprise**d," she said.

Mr. Crosswire looked **startled**. "Why, I know you. . . . You're Miss McWord, my grade-school★ English teacher."

"Yes, I am, Edward." She walked up the steps. "I'm glad to see your **memory** hasn't **fail**ed you—even if your **common sense** has."

"Miss McWord, I **assure** you I have every **bit** as much common sense as I ever did."

She stood beside him. "That may be true," she **admit**ted. "I see you haven't changed. You never were much of a reader. Can you **appreciate** how hard a writer works to **create** stories kids will like to read? Each story is like a **seed**, Edward. If a child reads one, the seed may grow into the **desire** to read another. That's something every writer hopes for."

Mr. Crosswire **cross**ed his arms. "Oh,

★ **grade-school** (= elementary school) 초등학교.

really? Miss McWord, you were **certainly** a **fine** teacher. But what makes you such an **expert** about what writers hope for?"

"Well, I'm a writer myself."

"Oh. I'm sure we're all **delight**ed to hear that." Mr. Crosswire **hesitate**d. "Anything we'd know?"

Miss McWord **straighten**ed Mr. Crosswire's jacket and **flick**ed some **lint** from his shoulder. "Nothing you've read, Edward, **consider**ing your common sense and all. But since you've asked, I'm the **author** of the Scare-Your-Pants-Off Club books."

"You!" said Mr. Crosswire, turning **pale**. He had a sudden **vision** of Miss McWord walking him down to the **principal**'s office.

"You?" said Arthur.

"Her?" Francine, Buster, Sue Ellen, and the Brain said together.

The woman **nod**ded. "E. A. D'Poe is my

pen name.★"

Muffy nearly **explode**d with excitement. "Ms. D'Poe!" she cried. "I'm your number-one fan! I have all your books. Could I have your—" Her parents **glare**d at her. "Oooops!"

She **clasp**ed her hand across her mouth as her parents **surround**ed her.

"You read them all?" said her father.

"And just when did you do that?" asked her mother. "Mary Alice Crosswire, you've got some **fancy** explaining to do."

"Uh-oh!" said Muffy.

"If you've read all of these books," said Mrs. Crosswire, "then **obvious**ly it wasn't one of them that gave you the **nightmare**. What was it?"

"Um, well . . ." Muffy hated it when her mother sounded like a **detective**.

★**pen name** 필명. 글을 써서 발표할 때 사용하는, 본명이 아닌 이름.

"Just a minute, here," said Mr. Crosswire. He **stare**d at Muffy. "Now I know who ate my quart★ of Haasen-Pfeffer ice cream."

"And then was **afraid** to admit it," said her mother. "Mary Alice, you know eating like that gives you bad dreams."

"We're very **disappoint**ed in you," said her father.

"And I'm disappointed in you, too," Muffy's mother said to her husband. "What were you doing with a quart of that ice cream, anyway?"

"Well, I . . ."

Arthur almost smiled. Muffy and her father were both standing with their heads **hang**ing low. They looked very much **alike**.

Miss McWord cleared her throat. "I hate to **interrupt** a **promising** family **squabble**,

---

★**quart** 액량의 단위 쿼트. 1쿼트는 1/4갤런, 약 1리터이다.

but we've still got some business to **settle**. Edward, maybe you can take your foot out of your mouth★ long enough to listen to one of my stories. That way you can make an **inform**ed decision about who should be reading them."

"Oh. Yes. Excellent idea."

At this **particular** moment, anything was better than **facing** his wife.

★ **take your foot out of your mouth** 실언을 했다고 할 때 'put one's foot in one's mouth'라는 표현을 사용하는데, 직역하면 '입 안에 발을 집어넣다'는 의미이다. 본문에서는 이와 반대로 실언을 수습한다는 의미에서 '입에서 발을 꺼낸다'고 표현하고 있다.

Chapter 10

*"And since that night, nobody has **dare**d to **steal** anything from the **haunt**ed hamburger **stand** again."*

Miss McWord put down her book.

The crowd **clap**ped and **cheer**ed. Among the loudest fans was Ed Crosswire.

"Well, Daddy?" Muffy asked.

He **sigh**ed. "I guess I shouldn't have tried to stop you kids from reading books without knowing the whole story myself."

"Maybe," said Miss McWord, "you have changed some, **after all**, Edward."

"So can we have our books back, Mr. Crosswire?" Arthur asked.

"I will **disband** PAWS on one **condition**," said Mr. Crosswire.

Everyone fell silent.

"And that condition is?" said Muffy.

"That Miss McWord will read us another story." Mr. Crosswire looked at her. "Please?"

"Yes!"

"Another one!"

"All right!"

Miss McWord smiled, something she didn't do very often. She **crack**ed open another book.

*"No one in the **village** knew why the old man lived all alone, deep in the dark woods. Only the animals of the **forest** knew his secret. . . ."*

Arthur sat back and closed his eyes as a **familiar chill crept** up his **spine**.